For Brian
—K.B.

For the grandmothers: spoilers
of children, saviors of parents
—B.H.

Thanks and applause for
our colorist Jo Rioux.

Library of Congress catalog card number: 2014934804
ISBN 978-0-06-228596-6

Book design by Victor Joseph Ochoa
15 16 17 18 19   SCP   10 9 8 7 6 5 4 3 2 1   ❖   First Edition

GRAN on a FAN

by Kevin Bolger

illustrated by Ben Hodson

HARPER

An Imprint of HarperCollinsPublishers

Gran   can

Gran in a can.

Gran

fan

Gran on a fan.

Gran

van

Gran tans on a van.

cat

pat

Gran pats a cat.

cat

Matt

Take that, Matt!

Pets get wet.

Pets in nets.

Pets at the vet.

Nell

well

Nell fell in the well.

Nell yells . . .

and yells . . .

and yells. . . .

Oh well.

chimp

bib

Chimp in a bib.

kid

crib

The kid slid
out of his crib.

16

chimp

Mrs.

The chimp
kisses the Mrs.

King Ding-a-Ling

King

King clings.

King swings.

18

King flings. . . .

Ping!

Bing!

Ding!

King in a sling.

Pop

tots

mob

boss

bomb . . .

The mob robs a shop.

Pop jogs by the shop.

Pop stops.

cops

The cops spot Pop.

Pop jogs off.

"Stop that pop!" say the cops.

"Do not stop, Pop! Do not!" say the tots.

Dog

Dog spots the mob.

The cops got Pop.

But Dog got the mob.

Pop got off.

The mob did not.

The sub was Pup's.

Mutt jumped in.

The sub came up.

"Want more fun?"
asked Pup.

Yup.

Mutt said, "Yup."

Pup jumped in.

Pup tugged the plug.

That was too much
fun for Mutt.

Try these words again....

Short a:

can, fan, Gran, tan, van
cat, Matt, pat, that

Short e:

fell, Nell, well, yell, help
get, jets, nets, pets, vet, wet

Short i:

clings, flings, King, sling, swings
bib, crib
kid, slid
kisses, Mrs.
chimp

Short o:

mob, robs
Dog, jogs
cops, Pop, shop, stop
spots, tots, got, not
bomb, boss, off

Short u:

scrub, sub, tub
plug, tug
fun, clung, spun, sunk, under
Pup, up, yup
but, Mutt
jump, much, suds

well

Nell

Nell gets out of the well.